GERD BRANTENBERG

What Comes Naturally

Translated and revised by the author

The Women's Press

First published in Great Britain by The Women's Press Limited 1986
A member of the Namara Group
34 Great Sutton Street, London EC1V ODX

Reprinted 1987

First published in Norway as *Opp Alle Jordens Homofile* by
Gyldendals Forlag in 1973, and by Aschehougs Forlag in 1984.

British Library Cataloguing in Publication Data

Brantenberg, Gerd
What comes naturally.
I. Title II. Opp alle jordens homofile. *English* 839.8'2374[F]
PT8950.B7/

ISBN 0–7043–5001–7
ISBN 0-7043-4003-8 Pbk

Typeset by MC Typeset Limited, Chatham, Kent
Reproduced, printed and bound in Great Britain by
Hazell Watson & Viney Limited,
Member of the BPCC Group,
Aylesbury, Bucks

Contents

Acknowledgments

This was my first work of fiction and it was written in secrecy. I'd like to thank Ulla Simonsen, Copenhagen, for its being written at all – the way it is: I think that the book is very much a product of our friendship and the political consciousness that we shared.

For the English version of the book I owe a lot to Gillian Hanscombe, London, who went through the manuscript with me and brushed up the language.

Note on the terms
homosexual/homophile

Until the Gay Movement started in Scandinavia around 1970 the term 'homosexual' was the only term in common use. Coming of age in the fifties and sixties therefore meant this was the word you had to identify with. The gay political pioneers, however, introduced the word 'homophile' to draw attention to the fact that loving people of the same sex is not only a sexual matter – it concerns your life as a whole. The term became widespread and commonly accepted, and is the general term used nowadays in political debates. This writer feels it has become a kind of euphemism and therefore retains 'homosexual' as the genuine term, and uses 'homophile' with a tinge of irony. The word 'lesbian' is in the Scandinavian languages an even later coinage.

ONE

I'm not a queer, if that's what you think

You've asked me. You'll get an answer.

I haven't asked *you*. But you're normal, you say. It's abnormal to ask normals. Did you ever receive a form by post asking you to fill in, in the proper places, why you were normal? How you first understood that you were normal? Or whether you had any problems being normal: a) in the family, b) at work, c) among friends? Your parents' income and property, brothers and sisters and housing conditions in childhood, and whether you believed that these circumstances had any influence on your development as a normal person? And when, for the first time, did you accept that you were normal?

Do you have difficulties admitting to other people that you are normal? And do you at present live as a normal and have contact with other normals: a) exclusively, b) sometimes, c) never?

No? You've never been asked such questions? Even I don't ask them of you. That's because I find myself much more interesting. I'm followed everywhere by a perpetual question mark. How can I possibly avoid thinking that I'm *extremely* interesting?

My first mistress – well, please excuse the expression, but is there really such a thing as a neutral expression for a woman? – had short, dark hair and blue eyes. You can't imagine how wonderful it was, finally, not have to go to bed with a man.

No one forced me? Are you saying that no one forced me to do that? Really?

Anyway, her name was Gunnhild, and I didn't like her name. You know how these things are. Don't you? But that wasn't the worst thing about it. The worst thing was that I didn't like her nose. There was probably nothing wrong with it from a photographic model's point of view, but it struck me as being strangely flat. And a little too long. Yes, long and flat. That may sound trivial, but as a matter of fact it gradually became more and more important. As our relationship grew, Gunnhild became more and more nose. The more we quarrelled, the more I saw of her nose. By and by it became the most striking feature of her arguments.

But I'm starting at the wrong end. First there was the romance. The first time I met Gunnhild and her nose was in the wonderful month of May, when all the birds were a-chirping, if you remember the song. In the morning. And the sun was shining and the grass was green. Prospects, prospects. By the way, I had one of my depressions at the time. I have one of them now, too. And I had had another depression just before the one I was in when I met Gunnhild. My life is actually made up of a series of periods of depression, one succeeding another. Just play any pop tune for me – 'What happened to / The world we-e knew?' by Stevie Wonder, for instance, play that one – and I can tell you exactly which period of depression I was in at the time it was popular. The realm of song memories. Beautiful and devastating.

I can't say I met her in a bar in Casablanca. Why should I? Who ever gave anyone the idea that one ought to meet one's first lesbian love at a bar in Casablanca?

No, I met her on the Oslo tram going from the centre of

2

the town to Sognsvatn – and it's not even very radical to despise that 't' in Sognsvatn.* But apart from that, I'm rather Marxist. You know, I imagine that if we had had a different society from this prestige-ridden pop-community, I wouldn't be sitting here churning out this trash.

My plan was that this was to be the end of my story. But now I've told you already. Now you know.

We began talking because we knew a third person, and that third person introduced us: she was studying psychology, and she was the kind of person who always introduces people to one another, even on the tram. A typical contact-making person, whom I envy because I am not like that myself. On the contrary, I always do my best to make other people feel a bit out of place. Then I feel so 'in' myself. You know, when there's someone at a party who doesn't dare to speak, and who doesn't have the foggiest notion what the others are talking about, I try to give the impression that I know a hell of a lot about the subject discussed, so that the outsider understands how inside I am. I do this without consciously knowing it, of course. It just comes naturally. The art of drawing the conversation into the areas of your own knowledge. Have you noticed it too? One must always take care that the conversation doesn't slide into areas which one doesn't have a clue about, or hurry to change the subject before it's too late, before one gets involved in a discussion of the medieval mystery of light.

Well. This third person – a woman – saw it as her primary aim to fight the lack of contact between the existing members of humanity. The idea had cropped up about that time, by the way. Alienation was just becoming fashionable. So she introduced us, and she even invited us to tea. The result was actually a hugely successful contact. We were already in the

*'Water' in Norwegian is either *vann* or *vatn*. *Vatn* is the more popular form, and is thus regarded by some to be the politically more radical term. [Translator's note]

middle of the romance.

When Gunnhild and I went home, we didn't go home. Something had happened between us. The inextinguishable lesbian spark. You've surely heard about it? The one that was first ignited at Lesbos, because Sappho was so sad every time a young woman left the academy that she wrote her a poem. Fancy being sad because someone leaves! Perverted, that's what I call it. Don't you? That's what the history of literature also called it, and what it tried to conceal for centuries. In vain. Oh, so in vain.

This was the beginning of the disease that was soon to spread to the whole of western civilisation. Two women are capable of loving each other. Help! Egyptian women, for instance, were not lesbian in the least. Egyptian history is too old for that. But who knows what the pyramids conceal? Moreover, have you heard the theory that the queen who was buried in the Oseberg Viking ship had a servant woman with her in her grave because she was a lesbian? The archaeologists blushed so violently when they discovered it that they tried their best to cover it up. It shed such a peculiar light on our Viking ships – the pride of the Norwegian nation. But they didn't succeed. The truth nevertheless seeped out. One of the most outstanding examples of lesbianism in the Viking age. The lesbian wave that penetrated the Celtic Iron Ring and flooded up to the wild north. Put that in your pipe and smoke it. You don't smoke a pipe? Oh, I forgot. You're not a lesbian, of course.

The heritage of ancient times had not escaped Gunnhild and me. We noticed that as soon as we had got rid of the person who established our contact. (Her name was Tove, by the way.) We drank beer, of course. At a restaurant with a juke-box. Women hardly ever drink beer with each other in literature. But we did, just to spite literature. Because we knew immediately of course that we were in the middle of a lesbian novel.

4

At that time I lived in digs facing a horrible backyard. My view consisted of a fire wall. And the only thing I saw of Mother Nature was a rectangular section of sky, plus a couple of pigeons which strolled on the top of the wall. The imprisonment I felt living there was in itself enough to drive anyone into lesbian orgies.

As you might have guessed already, this room was not to witness my lonely activities that night. We stayed on at the restaurant until we realised that the only chairs that weren't on end on the tables were the ones we occupied. I went home with her.

We didn't go to bed with each other. We did that the night afterwards. And then we were together constantly for a whole week, and we were scared to death in case anyone understood why. We said, 'Do you think he has suspected anything?' and 'Do you think she has suspected anything?' and 'What do you think they would have said if they had suspected anything?' And we tried to mislead everyone who had the slightest chance of suspecting anything.

Conversations with friends and acquaintances ran approximately as follows:

'I hardly see you these days. What are you up to?'

'Oh, you know, life is more than hanging around in reading-rooms. . .'

'A-haaa! Speak up! Are you in love?'

(Mysterious smile.)

'Oh gosh, how exciting! What's his name?'

'No, drop it. I'm not telling you, anyway.'

'Why do you have to be so secretive? Has he got dark hair? Is it the man you were together with on the tram the other day?'

'Oh, h-i-m! Ha, ha. No, far from it.'

'That means there *is* somebody. Do I know him?'

'No, stop this guessing game. I'm not going to tell you. I don't know what's going to happen. I . . .'

(Sulkily) 'Well, if you don't want to, I won't bother you.'
Pause. Then suddenly:

'I just wondered . . . The girl you were with at the cinema the other day, who is she?'

'Wh. . .whom do you mean?'

'The one with dark hair, you know, and a sort of long nose?'

'Oh yes, I know . . .'

'She's not a student, is she?'

'No . . . '

'How do you know her?'

'I met her at a party a couple of months ago.'

Pause. Then suddenly:

'Please, can't you tell me who it is, the boy you met? I'm dying to know. . .'

It was a horrible time. Later, Gunnhild and I often spoke of what a glorious time it had been.

Particularly the first day. The first day became a journey that we travelled over and over again. We competed about who had become most attracted to whom first and how strongly. And when we'd first noticed it. In the end we agreed that we'd both noticed it first and strongest, immediately.

Our first day was a continuous source of renewal. Then the more we quarrelled and despised each other, the more we agreed how desperately in love we'd fallen on the day we met.

In our good periods we talked about all the things we'd talked about on the first night. We talked about how we'd talked until five o'clock in the morning, and spent about five hours avoiding *it*. Until finally I said I believed I was *homosexual*.

Shock! Horror! It had been said, and the roof didn't cave in. The word had escaped my lips, and her face and body didn't fall apart in terror. She was still sitting there! She was

6

sitting there with the same expression on her face as before. She saw me. She could see me, even though I had said *it*. She didn't disappear. The room didn't disappear. The house remained standing. The street lights still shone. The even burr of traffic from the Trondheim Road was still to be heard. Oslo prevailed. The earth went round the sun. The solar system didn't fall out of the Milky Way. The clock ticked. I was there. My hands were there, my shoulders, knees, hair. She saw me. She had heard *the word*, and still she saw me.

Do you know something? I've often thought that the awful thing, the really excruciating thing, is that the world does *not* go under at such a moment. It remains, mercilessly unchanged, to be lived in.

What an idiot. May I introduce myself? I – twenty-four years old, a student – I believed, for twenty-four years, that the world would change because I uttered a word.

Do you know what she said? When I'd uttered the unutterable? She looked at me, and she really had such pretty blue eyes to look at me with, and then she said, 'You know, you're not the only one.'

I gathered it was a theoretical statement which could be verified in various works of science and art. No one had ever denied to me that there was such a thing as homosexuality. Homosexuals were bohemian-like, artistically inspired characters, who lived in attics with sloping roofs and skylights in London, West Berlin and Paris. Particularly Paris. Nearly all of them were men. But some of them were women. Mostly in the circles round Françoise Sagan and among the Existentialists. Perhaps I would meet a tall, slim girl one day – with short, dark hair – who painted pictures à la Van Gogh, and with whom I could live in such a gallery and lead a secret lesbian life.

But this was so distant and unrealistic that I had a far more realistic dream. I dreamed that I cut my hair short and dressed up in men's clothes and went out to a strange city where no one knew me and tried my luck. Greta Garbo had managed it in *Queen Christina*. That was promising. The person I really was should be wiped out. The person I really was couldn't get the person I really wanted.

I'd come to realise, you see, that if I wanted to attract a woman, I had to be a *man*.

In Norway the chances were small. There were a few homosexuals in Oslo, and they were mostly engaged in the theatre and had Adam's apples. In my little home town of Fredrikstad – a town of 13,000 inhabitants at the time – there was *one* homosexual. He was the object of great giggling in the streets, because he was cheeky enough not to conceal it. The homo of the town. A man. There were no lesbians in Fredrikstad.

When I asked my mother what the matter was with that man, she said (sensible as she was, but then she was from a family of actors herself) that he was a homosexual, which meant that he preferred men to women. I was about ten years old then, and I stood at the kitchen window and thought: I wish I could go up to him and say he could have my gender, because I didn't need it, and then I could have his. I considered it was a stupid trick of nature that such a thing was impossible.

Twelve years at school, mostly passed in the mindless fifties, did not include one minute of sex education. That was a great leap forward compared to my mother's schooldays, when sex education consisted of skipping the sixth commandment. Until she read Evang's *Information on Sexuality* secretly, she conscientiously believed that she was the only person in the world who masturbated. But maybe I ought to be grateful that we had no education on these matters, for I avoided hearing from the teachers that I was a pervert.

But I had a lively girlfriend who suddenly said to me one day, 'Do you know something? I get mad about girls, too.

Not just boys. Do you?'

'Yes.'

And then we rode around on our bikes and were mad about girls *and* boys. Oh, happy, happy childhood days!

Finn Grodal was a man who didn't want to risk his real name, but he had written a thick book on the subject called *We Who Feel Differently*. There was a copy of it in our library, and it was published when I was in my senior class at school. But we were too grown-up to talk about such things by then. Still, when I heard the title I had no doubt that it concerned me. It turned out that the book was only about men. 'We' did not include me. Not even in this obscure book that no one talked about did I have any existence. 'We' were a number of unhappy men.

But there were actually some homosexual women during the First World War. One of them had written a book about it called *The Well of Loneliness*. It turned out that the main character was a man in the shape of a woman. It was just as well written as a short story in a popular magazine, and it moved me just as deeply. Her great, unforgivable fault was that she wasn't a man – biologically – and therefore she had to renounce the woman she loved. She realised herself that this was morally right.

And after all these years I was sitting here saying to another human being that I *believed* I was a homosexual . . .

What? I wasn't the only one? Hm. As if I didn't know! I was so spellbound by my own volcanic eruption of *the word* that I didn't for a moment stop to think about what she meant.

I went home along the tram rails and thought endlessly while the birds chirped. Ti-ti-tu, ti-ti-tu. A silent, light, green, summer morning. The most beautiful thing on earth. I was terribly sad.

The next day I discovered that no matter what I decided to think of, I thought of Gunnhild. I thought of her eyes. I thought of what she thought about me. Did she think about me? I thought that I wished she were here now. I took her hand. Stroked her hair. Then I kissed her. I became totally confused. No. She put her arms round my shoulders. Then she kissed me. I rolled scene after scene. Back again. Made a new one. By the afternoon I'd thought so much about her that the very thought of contacting her seemed a distant fable. I played Brahms' Violin Concerto in D-minor at full volume while I drank three pints of beer and conducted the last movement. Then I went out, head over heels, hired a cab and went home to her.

When the taxi driver stopped in front of the house I had thought of about five hundred times during that day, I asked him to turn round and drive me back into town. I was convinced that he'd guessed the truth immediately and that he was sitting there driving along thinking, 'So she *is* a homosexual, that's what she is.'

I went into a restaurant and ordered a pint. What had I imagined? That she'd been sitting there all day waiting for me? Me – a woman hunting another woman. What excuse did I have to go running up there?

I started thinking of all the mistakes I had made. I'd told her how lonely I'd been. How prostrate with love for a girl who was two years older than me I'd been at school, a prostration which lasted for many years, even though I never talked to her. The more I thought about it, the more mistakes I remembered.

I had even told her about Tove. Well, you see, even though I think that psychology students are trendy on principle, I'd been madly in love with Tove for a long time. For four years, to be exact. On my knees. But I hadn't had a chance. Not because she didn't like me. On the contrary. She was so fond of me, she said. So that was that.

Tove was in everything I did, read, sang and talked about through various of my periods of depression. Life, the stars, eternity, and the transitoriness of all things had meaning only in her presence.

Now it was over. It was ages ago. I hadn't been in love with Tove for a long time now. It had developed into a deep and lasting friendship, which is much more valuable in the long run. I had repeated this to myself every day for about a year now. My feelings for Tove were far more relaxed and lasting than the feelings I had had for her the first year I knew her. Because then I had thought about her every day.

I had gone to a psychologist. My god! I had even told Gunnhild about that! Something that I'd never confided to anyone before. Help! I want to go home to my mother and hide under the blankets and never say another word till the end of time.

The psychologist had not understood a word of what I'd said. But I can't say that I helped him much. On the contrary, I tried my utmost to mislead him. The thing was, I was embarrassed. I knew far too well why I'd come. The closer I got to the truth, the more I tried to veil it.

But my psychologist was more of a psychologist than I'd reckoned with. Suddenly he said, 'Do you know something? I think you ought to be more open to men.'

It was like a pistol shot. I had no idea what I'd said that had revealed my soul so completely.

There; he had me taped, didn't he? What was I going to say to that? He left me speechless. I shall never forget how speechless he left me and how exactly he'd had me taped.

That was grist to his mill. This was no ordinary trendy person that I had in front of me. It was a chief spirit in the realm of trendy performances. He told me that what I felt was probably real enough to me, but that didn't mean that it really was real. It was probably only a passing phenomenon. I was young. I had the future before me. (I suppose he was referring to the millions who had their future behind them.) I shouldn't jump to conclusions.

Between you and me, 'What the stars say' couldn't have put it more precisely.

He said that the person I felt so strongly attached to (i.e. Tove), ought to be put in the background. It would lead nowhere. I myself was the best proof of that. Didn't I agree? Yes. I was frustrated, he said. I shouldn't let fear get hold of me, he said.

At long last I managed to mutter that I'd actually always felt most attached to girls, and I couldn't remember one single time . . . 'That's post-rationalisation,' he said. (After all, he spoke to an academic person.) Dangerous, dangerous. I should be careful not to make decisions too quickly. Many women were twenty-five, even thirty, before they found somebody who suited them. And I was only twenty. Everything would be all right. I shouldn't be too pessimistic.

But I *had* found somebody who suited me! I had found her over and over again! The world was full of people who suited me. And I never stopped finding them. Why did I have to find someone else? The world was full of people who didn't suit me, too. Why did I have to choose one of them?

But I didn't say this, of course. I hardly thought it, I think. On the contrary, I felt deeply grateful. Oh, thank you so much, Mr Psychologist! Is it really true? Is it really not quite certain that I am a homosexual after all? Oh, comfort and joy! Comfort and joy. What a relief! Then I may not have to be together with women, after all? Oh, I'm so glad to hear it. I feel relieved now. Perhaps I don't have to be a pervert. Perhaps I shall be as normal as the normals when I grow up? Oh, spiritual adviser, I rejoice in thy memory:

Psychologist, I thank thee
For the balm you gave me
I am not a deviant queer;
Towards a husband I will steer.

So I just had to leave and realise how wrong I was loving somebody. If one loves somebody, it has to lead to something. If I love someone, I'm afraid of what it might lead to. I must be led on the right track, otherwise it won't lead to anything. Love between two women isn't anything.

Just a passing phenomenon, lasting twenty years.

And now I'd told Gunnhild everything about this super-defeat in my life. In great detail. I decided I would never dare to see her again for the rest of my life.

Then I paid the bill and took a taxi to her address for the second time. Nobody fainted when our eyes met. At that moment I realised what she'd meant when she said I wasn't the only one. I fell over her on the sofa. She said she thought we ought to get to know each other a little more closely first.

So we did.

TWO

The wonderful world of theory

The first stage – good lord, what a strain! In the Society of Socialist Students I'd learned that it was bourgeois to turn the light out. As for us, we were so bourgeois that we didn't even have the nerve to embrace each other without having turned out the light. Then we didn't have to see how peculiar it was with two girls. Because it is. Don't deny it. I can see that you're trying to put up a front, saying that you don't think it's peculiar in the least. But that's a lie. You aren't so tolerant. You can't be more tolerant than I was. And I was pretty intolerant of what I felt and did. But I did it.

I did it in spite of the fact that everyone knows that two girls don't fit together. They don't fit *into* one another, if you see my point. Don't pretend you never thought of that. You've been thinking it all along, while I've been telling you this long story. Just one question in your head, while I'm wringing my soul out for you in all its blasphemous details: *How do they do it?* That's the question. Am I not right? *How do two girls do it when they do it*? That's your central and haunting and never-ending question. I know you.

But as I've already told you: you've asked me and you'll get an answer. I always keep my promises. And this is a promising one.

Honestly, Gunnhild and I asked this question too. But we didn't have time to answer it before we'd answered it. Afterwards a thought popped up in all its majesty. *The thought of the penis.* The gospel of its inevitability had not left us untouched. Like most people in our cultural hemisphere we had not avoided its dogma. Something had to fit into something; if not, one can't do what one does. A kind of hand-in-glove theory. At the time when I went around on the surface of the earth trying to find an alibi for the crimes of my spirit, I had also stubbornly maintained that a man and a woman fit much better together – from the hand of nature. Nature provides everything wisely, according to the hand-in-glove principle. Not for one moment did it occur to me that nature had made *me*.

How did nature come to make me? No, no, no. Nature hadn't made me. I was just there.

Now there were two of us. Now we were two people on the surface of the earth who weren't there.

In such confused situations the advertising of certain unmentionable articles in the big dailies could be of great help. This was way back in the sixties, remember. And it's only afterwards that this decade has become known as a time of revelation. In short, we ordered a packet of obscure articles, hoping to find in it what we later learned goes by the name of a dildo. There wasn't one. So we set about making one ourselves. It became an impressive piece of architecture. The only trouble was, which one of us was to use it? It turned out that neither of us wanted to use it. And even more embarrassing, neither of us really wanted the other one to use it, either.

So why did we make it?

I shall let this question stand by itself. You can ponder over it in vacant hours. It was, of course, a gigantic misunderstanding. She had thought that I wanted to use it on her and vice versa, and neither of us had had the nerve to say, 'Now, listen – I wouldn't dream of . . .' We were so eager to be understanding. And sexuality belongs to the darkness, where hidden forces remain hidden.

The episode caused a confusion which was never cleared up. We had to ask each other who was the man and who was the woman in this relationship. At first I was convinced that I was the man; but then, so was she. Were we then really two homosexual males? Afterwards I realised that it was rubbish to see myself as a man when I was really a woman. After a while Gunnhild came to the same conclusion. So there we were, staring into the unknown. We were women wanting women.

And that didn't fit into anything we'd learned. The only thing that my civilisation had given me a chance to understand was this: since I want a woman, and not a man, I am a woman with a perverted desire to *be* a man.

Consequently I ought to be provided with a penis. I ought to want a penis. I ought to envy penises. I ought to steal through the cover of darkness towards the woman I want, artificial penis in hand, and conquer her. So says Freud.

As I mentioned, my relationship with Gunnhild soon faded. I think we were too eager. It was wonderful, as I immediately assured you, finally to be with another women. But we lacked something. And it wasn't the above-mentioned article that we lacked. We weren't in love. We were obsessed by each other, but we weren't in love. We knew this. Because both of us knew what being in love was.

We decided to part. The decision went like this: I said, 'I don't want to go on. We have to put an end to this,' and she cried and said, 'I can't stand it. We must go on,' and then we went on for some time until she said one day, 'This is no use. We have to call it a day,' and I cried and said, 'How shall I go on without you?' So we went on for some time. In this way the relationship lasted for seven months. Gunnhild said, 'We like each other. We're lucky to have found each other. We share the same interests. And we're perhaps the only ones in the world who feel like this. What shall we do if we leave each other?' I said, 'But we don't love each other. We've said to each other that we love each other. But it isn't true. We can't be together if we don't love each other.'

But later I thought: how do I know that she doesn't love me? I can only speak for myself. And what is love, anyway? Love is different when you just feel it in your heart and never speak about it, and never try to live with it – close to the one you love. The moment your love is realised, it becomes something else. What is love?

Perhaps I didn't know what love was. I only knew what it was to *be* in love. And I wasn't in love with Gunnhild. And I believed that to love was to be in love continuously for the rest of your life. All the books had told me that. They ended when life began.

So we parted. And we mourned. We were lonely and full of sorrow. More sorrowful than we'd ever been. For now we knew. And not a single soul did we have to turn to. During all of the seven months that our relationship lasted we'd taken care not to behave in any way that could arouse suspicion. We squeaked up and down staircases and in and out of doors at each other's digs, we climbed through windows, stole our way to the bathroom in the middle of the night (when we got better acquainted we dealt with these needs on a bucket in the room, for safety reasons), we changed our voices when we called each other on the phone, and on Sunday mornings I used to steal out of the back door, and come back half an hour later to ask her landlady if Gunnhild was at home.

In other words, we didn't deviate very much from ordinary criminal behaviour. In our eagerness not to arouse suspicion we behaved utterly suspiciously.

The result of all this was that when we finally broke off, we had no one with whom we could share our sorrow. How could they ask, 'Are you sorry it's over?' when they never knew there had been anything? This was one peculiar consequence of our line of action that neither of us had thought of.

Moreover – if you finally had the courage to go to one of your friends and tell the truth about your perverted love life, how could you do that *and be unhappy*? No. The situation demanded that you came on like a beaming sun. Saying, 'I'm a homosexual' (we never said 'lesbian' at the time), and 'I am happy. I have now found a girl to love and she loves me'. Now, if you couldn't come and tell your friends that, what were you to say? You would just confirm them in their belief that being a homosexual is an unhappy fate. Chagrin d'amour – that's a heterosexual monopoly.

But never did I have a more intense need for someone to confide in than in the days after my love affair with Gunnhild had ended. I hadn't imagined this kind of loneliness before. It was a new and bitter kind of loneliness. A well of loneliness, perhaps. Yes. Perhaps that was the well of loneliness.

Gunnhild and I started being together again. We were the only lesbians in Oslo we knew of. Perhaps in the whole wide world. And anyway, neither of us really wanted to emigrate to a better place. We were Norwegian. We were Norwegian lesbians. We intended to remain so.

But in the meantime we'd both received a kind of shock. And in this shock condition we'd tried to figure out for ourselves what to do. Without knowing that the other one sat in her lonely room thinking exactly the same thoughts. Where do I go now?

I remembered that one of my student friends had once giggled about a Danish magazine called *The Friend*. It was at a student party where the male students got so drunk that they started asking each other in mock-female voices, 'You aren't *like that*, are you?' while they wriggled their behinds

18

and tried to dance with each other in exaggerated female style, oozing with joy and mirth, before, in typical male fashion, they tried to seduce one of the female students on the sofa. The female students were, of course, highly amused by the show, clapped their hands, and later hugged the virile necks that approached in order to confirm that it was all a show. Actually, this kind of entertainment was a favourite one in my student days. Strange, don't you think? Or are you perhaps a drag queen yourself? Well, many things have changed lately.

As it was, I used to sit and watch and pretend I thought it was marvellously funny, and consequently ended up in a corner with some gentleman who immediately started gasping for breath.

Well. I had at least got a piece of information that I thought could be useful. I went to the nice lady in the magazine kiosk. It was now or never. 'Do you have *The Friend*?' I said. 'Sorry', she said, and looked at me with friendly eyes. And I was convinced that they had instantly penetrated my deepest secrets.

I knew there was an organisation, but I didn't know where it was or how one got in contact with it. But I had ventured to buy the only Norwegian book on the subject – apart from the somewhat obsolete *We Who Feel Differently* – viz., Finn Carling's interview-based book *The Homophiles*. Now, you mustn't think that I went straight into Cammermeyer's Book Store on Carl Johan Street and said, 'I want Finn Carling's book *The Homophiles*, please.' For one thing, I pondered over it for about a fortnight and wondered if the shop assistant would think I was a lesbian, and assumed that a catastrophe would happen if she did think so. All the books would tumble from their shelves and the ambulance would be called – baa-boo, baa-boo, ho-moo, ho-moo through the traffic. No, I entered and tried to look as if nothing in the world concerned me, and said, 'Do you have any books by Carling?'

'A novel or an essay collection?'

This was a totally unexpected question. I blushed violently.

'It doesn't matter, as long as it's by Carling.'

My heart beat wildly and mercilessly. She disappeared. Soon she came back with *The Source and the Wall*. I already had this book.

'We only have *The Source and the Wall*, but we can easily ord. . .'

'No, no, that's all right. I'll take it,' I said, relieved to be let off so easily, paid in a hurry and went to the next book shop.

After this expedition I ended up with one copy of *The Homophiles* and three copies of *The Source and the Wall*.

Then I wrote a letter to Finn Carling and asked him where I could go. He wrote back, giving me the name of the Norwegian Society of 1948, with an anonymous address at the central post office in Vika. Gunnhild knew nothing of this, and I had no intention of letting her know. This was my business. I must be able to do something on my own. I wrote to the box number. Presumably they didn't meet at the box number. After an eternal period, a fortnight, the box number replied. The letter was signed by an equally anonymous-sounding name, 'I. Hansen', and I was informed that it was not possible to become a member of the society unless I knew one of the members. This was tricky. It was precisely because I didn't know any of the members that I wanted to become one. But the board could recommend me, the letter said. Therefore I had to meet some of the members of the board. I was asked to meet outside the Grand Café in the town centre with a copy of *Dagbladet** under my arm, at four o'clock in the afternoon, not the next Tuesday, but the Tuesday after that. Then somebody would come and pick me

*Dagbladet is one of the big national daily newspapers. [Translator's note]

up. Would I write and say if the time suited me, or should they find another date?

I wrote to the anonymous name (I.Hansen) at the anonymous box number and said that the time suited me perfectly, and thanked her/him/it so much for her/his/its answer. I was glad and excited. At long last I was going to meet other homosexuals.

I was twenty-three years old at the time. One may ask why I hadn't taken steps in this direction before. After all, I'd been in love with girls for as long as I could remember, and from the age of seventeen I had had a growing suspicion that I was queer. Six years is a long time, and time runs slowly in the tender years. To me it seemed I'd waited a lifetime. While my contemporaries trotted off to their love affairs, I could only stand and watch. So why hadn't I done anything before? Or would you say that the question is irrelevant? Would you, like my psychologist, rather have told me to bide my time?

Well, anyway, that wasn't the reason why I waited. I knew there was no time to bide. The reason was: why should I join an organisation for homosexuals in order to find someone I could love, when the one I loved was always nearby: one of my girlfriends at school, one of the students I went to classes with? I was always in love. What did I hope to find in an organisation for homosexuals? It was absurd. Still, I sought this organisation in the hope of finding my true love there – even though I had already found her. On the other hand, I reasoned, there has never been an assembly of about twenty women in which I couldn't find someone I liked. So I would probably like someone there, too.

Off I went. I took my stand outside the Grand Café in Oslo, not on the first Tuesday, but on the Tuesday after that, clutching that day's issue of *Dagbladet* under my arm – my precious entrance ticket to the beckoning underworld of our capital. I was far too early.

I was standing there curiously and guiltily looking at the people passing by and feeling that everyone was well aware of what that *Dagbladet* meant. As a matter of fact I was surprised that they seemed not to notice it. Extremely tactful. I looked at the crowd expectantly and wondered when the person with the anonymous name would turn up.

Then suddenly I saw Gunnhild coming up the street with a copy of *Dagbladet* under her arm. She stopped a few windows down from me. She was looking guiltily and expectantly at the crowd.

She hadn't seen me. I felt strangely dishonest, as if I'd deceived her. But if I had deceived her, she had deceived me, too. There we stood, having deceived each other.

There was no point in hiding, so I went up to her, and said hello. She looked at me and turned completely red, but before she had time to finish her blushing a woman who looked like a secretary came straight towards us and said, 'I gather you're the ones I'm supposed to meet here?'

I stared at her disbelievingly, feeling shattered. Was it possible that a lesbian could look just like an ordinary shorthand typist?

'Yes, I suppose so,' I said, totally embarrassed at having been found out.

'And you are the other one?' she asked Gunnhild. Gunnhild got into new fits of blushing and stammered an affirmative. Then we trotted off into the Grand Café.

I discovered that I was happy to meet Gunnhild here; after all, I was not alone in the world, even though the whole point was to be alone exploring the underworld.

In the café the secretary – was she I. Hansen? – ordered coffee. A lesbian woman ordering coffee! Now another woman appeared at our table, just as secretary-like as the possible 'I.Hansen', with a bouquet of flowers in her hands. She had obviously bought them for the other secretary. We talked. We talked! We had our first conversation with

22

lesbian women and nobody knew what we were up to. They told us they had had to check the criminal register to see if we were law-abiding citizens. They always did that with new members. Male homosexuality could be punished by one year's imprisonment* and they had to take precautions. Still, I found this a bit disheartening. Criminal register. Fancy that. But since they had found out we were law-abiding enough and they could see with their own eyes that we were good girls, they would recommend our membership to the board, and we were invited to join them at their next meeting on Saturday. We would have to take a train at a certain time to somewhere on the outskirts of Oslo, and there I. Hansen would pick us up.

'Who is I. Hansen?' I ventured to ask.

'That's just a name we use.'

Then they disappeared. We watched them go. 'I'm sure they were lovers,' said Gunnhild. 'Why on earth do you think so?' 'Because of the flowers,' said Gunnhild. But I thought she was exaggerating. People don't need to be lovers just because of some flowers.

I shan't bore you with a report of the long series of adventures that now lay before us . . . What? Was that what you came for? But this is a moral lecture, not a fairytale. You must always bear in mind that the purpose of this whole tirade is strictly moral. I want you to think, I want you to become a little less stupid than you are, I don't want you to look inside my bowels. And anyway, how do you know I'm not just telling you a pack of lies?

I'll tell you a pack of truths from the wonderful world of theory instead. Remember, we are the twilight women of the world; nobody really knows anything about us. We're easy prey, so to speak, to be hunted down by any theory that any man takes it into his head to believe in. It's called science.

*Paragraph 213 in the Norwegian Penal code. It was abolished in 1973 after pressure from the Norwegian Society of 1948.

I'm sorry to disappoint you, but, before the adventures, you'll have to listen to a lecture on the science of lesbianism. There are many interesting books on the subject. They all try to explain why there are such things as lesbian women. It's a headache that never ends.

We are told that in the United States of America women become lesbians because they are bored in the suburbs while their husbands are on incessant business trips to the big cities. So they turn to each other. Besides, there is the tradition from the Wild West, where there were so many men to each woman that the women got fed up with men and turned to each other instead. Haven't you seen all the films with lesbian characters in the Wild West? *Annie Get Your Gun* was just a discreet forerunner. 'A-doing what comes naturally.'

In Paraguay, on the contrary, they've always been at war with neighbouring countries, which means there is a big surplus of women, since most of the men have been killed in some war or other. Therefore it's quite natural that the many surplus women seek out each other for comfort and intimacy. This, of course, was also the case in Germany after the war. The lesbians in Germany have very deep voices.

In Sweden there are an awful lot of lesbian women, because in Sweden the women are so liberated that they realised long ago how stupid it is to be subordinate to men. But in Spain the women are so oppressed that they cling to each other to escape from their brutal husbands. In France the situation is very complicated. Here the women are oppressed because of Roman Catholicism, but, on the other hand, they're liberated thanks to Sartre and his almost-wife, or whatever you call it – Simone de Beauvoir, I mean – and this uncertain state of affairs has caused so much confusion among the women that they have become lesbians.

Apart from all this, one knows about various cases of lesbian excesses among the Indian tribes of North America,